W9-CMZ-086

TO CELEBRATE

THE BIRTH OF

JOHN C.
GENTILE

July 29, 1998

HAPPY BIRTHDAY!

The Surprise Picnic

John S. Goodall

MARGARET K. MCELDERRY BOOKS

An imprint of Simon & Schuster
Children's Publishing Division

Printed in Hong Kong
LC Number: 98-85143
ISBN 0-689-82359-2

Originally published by McElderry Books/Atheneum, 1977
Revised Jacket Edition, 1999
10 9 8 7 6 5 4 3 2 1